Tone Aaness is a Norwegian author, born in Oslo. She now lives and works in the north of Norway. Heavy winters and snow do not prevent her from writing about summers. Bright nights do not prevent her from remembering darkness. She is a human rights activist, a peace activist, and an environmental activist. She is also a performance artist and a classically trained painter.

To my two wonderful children, the only ones who really challenge my perception of the world.

To all those who do not see; and to those who see, avoid blindness.

Tone Aaness

Happy Belated Birthday

Austin Macauley Publishers™
London • Cambridge • New York • Sharjah

This is a work of fiction. Names, characters, businesses, places, events, locales, and incidents are either the products of the author's imagination or used in a fictitious manner. Any resemblance to actual persons, living or dead, or actual events is purely coincidental.

A CIP catalogue record for this title is available from the British Library.

ISBN 9781035853588 (Paperback)
ISBN 9781035853595 (ePub e-book)

www.austinmacauley.com

First Published 2024
Austin Macauley Publishers Ltd®
1 Canada Square
Canary Wharf
London
E14 5AA

Table of Contents

The Only Tourist in Bhutan

When she woke up, he was already gone—*Strange!* she thought—*He left his diary.* She was about to open and read it, or at least look at what it was about, when the phone rang. It was one of those old things, old-fashioned, as if there had been no industrial revolution in the ancient home of Sally Sparks, except bringing alliteration to the table. But she guessed that was her mother's will, calling her Sally to match up with the last name, the glittering one. She never felt much like it, though, but she was an old woman now, not likely to ever return to this shithole called earth if she could choose. But he had forgotten his diary, and she was not sure whether it was deliberate or just a terrible accident. The phone would never give up. She got out of bed and made her toes touch the exact spot of her slippers, which had been red from the start; they were fluffy and nice to wear on those cold tiles.

Sleeping nude was one of her addictions, a bit strange concerning the skin that she was in, curling into the shape of an elephant hanging from its own surface. She was folding her breasts like pockets now, and by the time she would be at the end, they would probably be rolling their own way into the yoga room. The phone was in the hallway, if she could call it a hallway; it was more or less the whole entrance of Chrystal

Palace and approximately 70 feet to the top of it. The house, or the palace, some sort of old-fashioned mansion, was a soap attraction of hers, really grand and kind of living its own life. Still, she had been in here for some years now, and it did not change; the hallway had its life too, like no other rooms were really needed in the house. During the first years, she even installed a bed to the right of the front door, not knowing exactly why, since none of her young lovers had arrived yet. The books surrounded the limited size of 120 centimetres on a gigantic shelf going up to the ceiling, as if it were some sort of library she could sleep in if she needed to, and most of the time, she was up here on the second floor anyway, in the bedroom section. The books were mostly paperbacks, but she had left some room for the first editions her lovers would bring back to her when they had started to come around. As if she were a collector and not their own vanity, they mirrored in her eyes. She always knew that she wrote for a reason.

She never had expected him to call her up every morning. It was a surprise to her, she was still trying to cope with it. He knew, as he had pointed out to her before, that she would be standing in her insects at the top of the hallway, leaning towards the commode. For some reason, she had that nudist thing going on in the top section, probably due to the long distance to the ground floor. They could not see her. She had a phone on the bedside table, but it was the one for the house; someone would have to set it over. The phone in the hallway section on top of the drawers was a private one; only a few people had that number. If there was something to look forward to, or if she was needed, that was where the ring would fly. Occasionally, she would change the number, but not that often anymore; she had learned to take them by the glance now. They were not all that brilliant anymore; in the beginning, they all had that fresh off the boat kind of innocence, but it lasted only for some small minutes before it changed appearance, and then that needy, greedy kind of thing would grow. Most of the time, it was like Bhutan; as long as you did not mix the cups, they did not either. She just changed the number when it was needed.

She loved the sound of his voice; it was brilliant, even before Barbara, the diary, came around. He had this strange sound to it, as if he were an undercover choir member. But she had not yet asked him because there were all these things happening every day; like a fairy tale of memories and houses, he had to get going. You see, we all have to earn our living in this world. As the apartments had become smaller, adapting to the clients, rising interest, less work, all those things that we don't really talk about the stories had become better. He had in person, believe it or not, shown her the meaning of saying something in one way when they are at the top of the peak and another when they are actually about to roll people into the non-glory glass room known to neighbours as the rumour of an accident. He had been there before himself. You could tell by the way he lived into it. You see, it is so hard to change by the standards, and it gets worse the more you grow into it. It was all in the Brexit exit national anthem, so everything was ecological or about sustainability, and then you could even sell one square metre on the idea of being a futurist. He was good at it, she had noticed. She had given him the job when he lost the other one, and he could explain everything quite exactly all the way to the hemisphere. The fortune of owning something small had occurred to a whole lot of them, and they just went into the future with brilliant eyes, knowing that they were really saving the planet Earth on their own personal level, their own private economy.

She was barely herself coping with the electricity in the house. You see, even water seemed expensive now, and on the streets, she could meet these people randomly, with a poster on a stick, like she was going back in time. They had written all that old-fashioned crap on the white cardboard. 'Take from the rich and give to the poor.' Like they were living in some Robin Hood era, but Brexit took too long, that was her conclusion. The rest they could argue about themselves. In the end, who needed to fly anyway? She was not keen on mixing into the stratosphere any longer, making global heating her own personal problem again. The Bhutan story was some years ago, and she had stayed a while in Italy first. It was an accident. When Corona came, they closed it all down. She barely had a way out, and while she was waiting for the visa, she just left on the first flight, walking her own way into that country. The silence had overwhelmed her.

The diary, she was not likely to open it. Still, she had done so just to see how he did this thing called privacy. 'Dear Barbara! I am not likely to come home anymore.' It was dated several months before he came into her life, and she was sure there was no Barbara, but still, she felt a bit amazed by the diary. Who would ever call a brown-skinned leaflet by the name Barbara, if that was the name of the diary? Strange on the one side, but he was such a namer. He even named the spectators that came for the houses, just for the reason to entertain her. There was Niemi and Noaster, Fifi and a friend, Big and his brother. She was surprised. He had glued in the Bhutan article about her on the second page. She was not sure if that was the meeting she wanted on the first two pages, after the Barbara thing. It became evident to her that he must have read about her before he arrived at her door.

It was an old article from 2021, during the Corona period, when she had travelled to Bhutan. It was before her green period really started to mix in with her everyday life and the makeover of the house. "It wasn't until I got here that I realised I was making history," she said in the article. "I was not expecting to get messages from people welcoming me and thanking me for coming to the country. It brings me to my knees." She had a gong gong drum in her hands—that sort of thing you cling to when you feel like making ohm[1] your new friend. She had felt it like this for some years now, and it did not change. There was one thing she had to remember about conflicts: avoid them.

---

[1] According to the Hindu tradition, the sound of Ohm represents the whole Universe.

It Was Expected to Be Marvellous

Not many came on the door wearing a fruit T-shirt. 'Fruit yourself, but don't be nuts.' It was right on time. She had felt a bit lonely since she arrived from the journey, and he was kind of the first real sign of life. The basket with fruit seemed so delicious, but there was something else. She had an intuitive feeling that he was a kind guy, which sometimes happened to her, that she would actually like to talk to. It was immediate. She invited him in, and he stayed the evening, out in the hallway section, with all the books, from floor up, in the 120 centimetres width of the bed, on top of the pillows and the bedcover. Gina served them tea, and they balanced the cup on the silver plate that Gina brought them on. She liked lying on the side of a stranger, discussing some randomness from The British Herold, which she had been reading undercover for the last six years. She did not want them all to think she was a smartass and all that sort of thing. It would have corrupted her audience and brought her sales down to nothing. At least now, she had a couple of flat ones a month, enough to bring in the wallpapers on the two rooms she was restoring. The living room and the dining area. It was expected to be marvellous. Vanity Fair new for sure, when they made the article, it was definitely going to be marvellous. She was wearing a dress that was the exact same pattern as the old wallpaper. Six years ago, or was it eight? Front page stuff. She knew not for sure, but it was definitely going to be marvellous. Even Theresa May had commented on it sometime during a lunch at the Planet, before Brexit took her off. It was when the agreement was on hold. Before they cancelled Germany. It was definitively going to be marvellous.

She really was wondering whether he would move in, but she did not ask him. It was not yet lunchtime. He left the basket behind, said that it was just the first job of his. She ate fruit all week, and the next time he came by, he only brought bananas. He said he forgot his basket last time and had to come back, but he did not want her to be without fruit for another week. So he brought the bag; it was pink, and he asked her to keep it till next time he would come around. Only this time, she started to wait for him.

The Hills of Oklahoma

"I will come by later, if you like," he said. The silence was always like this. He knew. You see, she could say no, and that was what was evaporating his voice. The uncertainty of a metaphysical breakdown, a suicide in the memory. He had been shivering for the last decade, some months now, was it, wondering if she would ever ask him to stop coming. He had already been up at seven, just to be sure that he could tell her a story before nine, which was at a maximum of sleep on her behalf. He knew. Then something had delayed him; it was already half past nine when he started to run the bell. His mobile phone was red before she took off the griff of the old fashioned phone in the hallway, installed to be connected still, believe it or not, to the phone lines—now hidden under the ground. It still existed a few of those antique objects. The phone was like herself. Then she answered back. He had thought of a million different stories to tell but bagged the wrong one. She never liked couples that quarrelled that much, and he had to make them make up in the toilet as he was filling out the contract on the world's smallest apartment. Sixteen square metres with a toilet and a shower curtain around the porcelain. It barely had a price. But it did not look like they had one either. When he started to murk around details of prices and small rooms, the phone fell off the drawer section and hit the wood top on the commode, and he felt a bang in his ear. She was standing, you see, with her bare ass on the hills of Oklahoma. It was only the stairs behind her. Hopefully, there was no one around to make her breakfast in the kitchen. They could watch her skin atonement from downstairs, and it would make a problem for later; freedom had certain aspects that only a few persons could understand. The chef was unlikely to be one of them. He felt upset by the dump smash, and he instinctively knew that the story was too long, summoning a soreness of depression; he sometimes liked to romanticise, but her house was too big. He knew. For that type of entertainment. She did not like that. Revolution was breathing them all down the line. You see, standard comes with a status. That was what they all found hard to forget.

Of course there were no couple; it was a young girl, nearly sixteen, looking for a place to study abroad. Her father had been on the phone from Greece, not that comedy type, and the sales took him maybe ten minutes. How often did that happen? But he did not want to tell her. The girl, who was too young to study anything at all, had strolled out of the room before he could even ask her name and left him with her father's number. Knowing that Sally was about to sell the Catalonian house with all its memory, just wanting her to have it done, the sooner the better, he invented this tremendous story about the lovers. Then he made the kitchen too small for a food lover, claiming there was nowhere for the air of Chili con Carne to escape after dinner. The dinner would never come out of the house. Normally, she liked that sort of thing, but not today; she seemed reckless, as if he had to advance to keep her attention. So he made them sleep together in the bathroom. They must have been standing up, he told her, since there was no room for sitting without having the door open. It was the first time he heard her smile through the cables, into the airy signals of his latest mobile phone, and it seemed real. He was happy, and before he was able to think through his actions, he had kind of popped the question, and here he was waiting for her to answer. Did she want him to come by? So many ways to ask a question like that, and he had chosen the least interesting one. The silence blushed through his veins, and he felt like his head had lost its voice.

Barbara was another kind of girl; she did not like to do anything on her own.

A Country of No Original Dreams

She had always liked travelling, but in the end, there were so many ways to travel. Sometimes she felt like she came from a country with no original dreams. Catalonia was different; she had met a young man. He was no more than 25, and his skin was like the fruit of a peach—no more, no less. His eyes were pale blue, and he did not speak much Greek to her; he claimed to be an Athenian. So she continued to speak Spanish, knowing that he probably was a bit short on money, but who was not on the short side in Spain these days? Every night out in the main street that week they had spent in Madrid;, the young girls from the close-by farms had come in to sell some jewellery. The truth was, they had to sell so much more. It made her sad.

Still, they did not want to print the article; the editor, Pierce Channing, said no on the phone. Too much fuss for Britain. They did not face that problem themselves, so she rather keep it Spanish he said. He was looking forward to the next pocket, though. Let the politicians face some real challenges before you hit them with the scandals this time, or will it all be fiction? He laughed; probably he had a hangover from last night's party. Who was the lucky one? It took her two days to have a street magazine in Madrid print the same news—not exactly El Pais, but it would do. She explained the main street situation in a way that most mothers could understand; at least, she thought so. She had her young lover read it through. Was he 25? She could have exaggerated, but on the other hand, he knew how to read. It was the first time she heard someone call her a genius, and he suggested the Gandhi method, knowing that something had to be made by cotton all over the world.

When he made love to her the second time after reading the text, he did it with a certain gentleness, as if he were sorry to say he was not Greek, but it did not occur to her anymore; she would not have taken him anywhere without being fluent in her own language, and especially not without knowing one of his father's friends. You see, Spain is like that; you would rather create intrigue in a well-known family than be killed at the door. She thanked him for the help; 200 euros was still affordable, and he was a student, too young to work more than a couple of nights at the hospital. It is always like that, she said to herself; the best ones also know how to do a bit of surgery.

30 Ways to Be a Good Mother

She had been the only tourist in Bhutan, he knew. It never occurred to him how it happened, but something had probably gonged through her brain at that time. He wished he knew what, or who. They had been isolated in their own homes for weeks, facing the Corona pandemic, and he remembered the quiet hills of Scotland better than his own parents. He measured the green tones of the tapestry and tried to find inspiration in the flowers. There was not much going on in there, and the quiet seemed to close him into a zone of no aligning truths. He stayed on the side of everything. Rolling the chair in and out of toilets for months. Barbara had a second problem now; her breathing was already heavy. They could not have the Corona coming around as well. For a while there, he was exhausted by routine. Nothing seemed to change except the weather. And then, the only tourist in Bhutan, Sally Sparks, was in the news. It must have been the one traveller at that point, so he read the article and felt that she actually gonged his brain too.

He was out of work until the fruit job came around. He just went down there, bought a basket and filled it up. That was how it came around. And it was all ecological, in a strange sense—you know the way it becomes the e for ecological in whatever name that begins with e-stickers? He bought the stickers himself. It looked like everything had been grown with the utmost care, sticker e on the apples, on the grapes, on the clementines, on the oranges, and he even stuck one on a cucumber. He had to wait two days for the T-shirt, though.

The 'Print and Pack It' made some fuzz about him coming around to get it. "I mean, they said, we send? People don't come around." Sorry, excuse us, they added, all those things, but they still said no, even when he was at the door or in the window. There would be no T-shirt. He would have to wait for the mail said the guy with the brown floppers—that was what he would call that sort of thing—some stringed spaghetti hairdo that would flop around his airs in a brownish manner. Not exactly God's gift. He had not shaved his rooties either. It looked like there were trunks coming out. The cheeks were a forest on their own, with no leaves coming.

He did not dare to put his hand in the gap between the window and the wood. He did not know what kind of type the other guy was; maybe he would be a loony, some sort of banging hands kind of dude that would break his fingers. So he did the only thing he could do: he took out a hundred, hundred pounds—the last one of his—and said that he could keep the change if he just gave him the T-shirt. Something seemed to pop into the guy's mind because he called out for help. "Winnie, get that shirt coming, will you? Enough fuzz with that kid! It is the third time he's outside my window this week."

"Does not matter; send is what we do." Someone was shouting on the inside.

"I know, but he is ordering another thousand if he likes the material."

"Thousand?" he heard. "Well, I understand what you mean." It took the voice a couple of minutes to come up to the window. "Not bad..." he said, "...another thousand. You better get back here before Monday." He pointed a finger at him. The other guy was still holding his hand flat, pushing it south as if to tell him where to keep the money. He got the shirt; it was this type of thing you knew was the exact measurement; it cropped around the body like the top of a jumpsuit.

He had been working out for months. It would fit the mould.

He changed the T-shirt in the car. He told Barbara she had to stay by herself most of the day. He bought her a book, '30 Ways to Be a Good Mother'. It was that sort of thing that interested her. He could do nothing about it. He had, in the early days, asked her if she wanted to adopt. She told him no because she did not want to wheel the baby around in the house. He had not expected that answer. So he stayed silent for weeks. Later, he bought her the dog. It was, of course, very clear to him that it all happened after he had met Sally. Even the dog was blond and curly; it had the ridiculous name Sparks. He could not remember who invented the name, but after the dog was baptised, there was no way back. Sparks would be called by the name. Out in the park, she let him free, and then he came back whenever she would call for him. If it is a divorce, he often told her, you can keep the dog. It is not my type of thing. Barbara used to laugh; divorce is not my type of thing; she nodded back. You could have the dog.

To Compare Things

"So you are married?" she said.

"To a woman in a wheelchair," he answered back. And I am 70, she wanted to say, but she did not like to compare things.

"So the logo is new?" she said, looking at his T-shirt. He was still wearing it. He smiled at her.

"What is it for lunch?"

"I will call up the butler…" she said, "…or no one has a butler anymore, really. Is it something politically incorrect about that expression?" He said it would depend on the food. "Don't get out of bed!" she said. She took the ancient thing and called down to the kitchen. The new guy was up in a second.

He wore a black, shiny suit and a white, stiff shirt. He had white gloves and a towel over his arm. The bow was made of black silk. He was about 30 years old, a beautiful African boy. He was surprised. "Where is Charlie, the old guy? He was such a wonder at his things," he said when the fellow had left the room.

"I felt like a change," she said, looking at him.

"Ohh!" he said.

"It is not such a big deal carrying some eggs and bacon," she added. "I think he will be fully capable of it."

He did not ask about having the diary back. She probably had read it all anyway, and he did not want to remind her too much about that thing. But he started to look for it, though; sometimes he would lean on the side to move out a drawer, for instance, in the bedside table. "Are you looking for something?" she said. He kept it light, as she normally found so amusing.

"I am looking for myself, darling!" he would say, laughing. He decided to stay without shirts for a while. The last one would probably print his brain forever. "What goes around, comes around." Not exactly the thing he was looking for anymore.

So Peter had come up with eggs and bacon, and they could all three have stayed in bed, but he did not want to tell her about that feeling. Too much fuzz about that guy anyway; he wore those gloves as if they would still be part of the British Commonwealth kind of thing. He never liked supremacy much. When Peter the 'butler' put down the coffee cup on his bed table, he bowed down and whispered into his ear at the same time, "I needed the money!" He did not listen much to the conversation between them after that. Sally had this warm cling to her voice when they communicated. He could definitely tell that he was younger than him, maybe by a year or two.

Peter 'the butler' left the room; the eggs were still warm after going by the food elevator two floors up. He could not tell whether the 'butler' or the guy, so to speak, had gone by the stairs or taken the one for human beings on the side. He was sure about the food, though, due to the toast as well. It was still a lukewarm feeling of heat on the bread-side top, as if to tell him that size mattered. The food elevator was approximately a half-metre, and it would count for the whole heating process of every kind of egg and bacon; as long as the servant would keep the cloaks on, the heat would stay in the food.

“He has a doctorate from Cameroon,” she said to him. “I will teach him English in between the guests.”

“Good idea!” he said. He had not touched his coffee yet, did not feel like being too awake. He had been thinking about a story to tell her, but he was still processing the Catalonian house that she had not sold. She would soon need the money.

“I was thinking about moving the opening party for my next book to the living room,” she said. “I think it will be ready by then. They are installing the crystals for the ceiling right now.” He had not ever seen a carpenter come around, but he nodded his limbs, down to the last toe of his.

“Do you think he could look at my back?” he said. “I have this kind of pain in my spine.” She turned towards him, smiling a bit too politely.

“He is not that kind of doctor, darling.”

Every Kind of Original

He said it was a piece of cardboard, nothing to worry about. "Yes," she said, looking at him. She wore those gold frames that she often used to see the details in the closeups. "I know you see it that way, but Peter bought it at the Vintage; it is an original." He looked at her. "When you threw it in the trashcan, you damaged it. It had some fat on it. I don't know how to remove it without ruining the colours."

He looked at her. "I can ask Barbara; she likes that kind of thing. She is much into details."

She took off her glasses and gave them to him. "I don't know if you see that rather big, dark thing that grew out in the red area. If you put them on, you might see the detail of it." He never liked using her glasses; they did not help him much. He got that blurry kind of thing coming, and no detail would ever occur to the front of his irises. He could not tell if it was red or brown or what happened in the zone of the cardboard painting at all. It was all a mystery. It was kind of all things mixing up in it. He just did not want to tell her about the glasses. It was a thing they shared together.

He liked sharing. But he could not see a thing. He really did not catch the point of it.

“Turn it around!” she said, still watching him. “Do you see the signature? It is a Munch, a lost version of *The Scream*. It is his most famous painting. One of the versions went for 120,000,000 at Sotheby’s.” He took off the glasses and looked at the painting.

“Ohhhh…!” he said. He did not feel like bringing Barbara into it any longer. She was still watching him with that strange look.

“Maybe…” she said very slowly, “you should rename your dog.”

A Child of One's Own

He said she could keep the dog, but she did not want to. She said that the dog was not the sort of thing that she would keep. Then he said that she could at least change the name. She said that he gave her the dog and invented the name himself. He could keep it and change the name, but with her, it was Sparks. And if the dog had to have a first name, she would have called it Sally, even though it was a boy.

She spent so much time by herself that she had learned how to make waffles, which was not really a British tradition. She told him it was due to the Brexit. They would have to change habits. This was 'a continental'. They would have to stay more on the European side from now on. He could choose, she said, with ice cream on the side, but there would be nothing wrong with 'egg and bacon' lined up on the plate as well. She had read it somewhere before she had Suffington buy the iron. It was kind of too good to be true. They had waffles for lunch every day now, and still, he was not there. He could not possibly know if she was able to make the best ones. He had nothing to compare with. Normally, there was nothing left. That was his sort of life now. She was amazed by how good she was on her own, but she did not want to divorce. She could even shower now using the long scrubber down her spine. She was too good to be true; all her neighbours said so too, too good to be true. Out the front door on her own, bringing the dog on her own and driving up to the park on her own. She was like a one human car on her own. And there on the bench, she would sometimes meet Suffington, a rather nice guy from France. He would sit on the bench, looking for her. He liked waffles, so he bought the iron, and they had their first lunch the fourth week. Before that point, he only cleaned the house.

Then he started to meet her out on the bench once a week, but as he liked waffles all that much, he started to come around every day, and now that Dora from Mexico had overtaken the job, they enjoyed the conversations instead of all that practical stuff. He normally had an hour, so the dough had to be ready before ten or so. It was really something to get up for.

The table was ordinary, just about 60 centimetres, due to the range she had, and they had agreed upon keeping the iron on the second shelf in the sideboard cabinet in the kitchen. It was easy to handle. Dora would often like to come around during lunch too, but she had made an effort to make her come at two o'clock. It was the hardest work she had ever done. You see, Dora was that kind of girl who knew exactly what she wanted, and she had a child of her own.

They Were All in the Grave, Sort of

The last shirt was different. He did not really mean to have it printed in the same store, especially since they were still waiting for 'the thousand-order'. He never came for more than one, but they had got to know his type of guy now, so they gave him the thing out of the window, but they had reported the fruit brand when he asked for the sticker, so he had to buy it somewhere else for the car if he would ever bother. When he asked for the last one, he wanted the text 'King of the Road', just to give Peter that strange butler feeling without being too clear about it.

But they did not do that; they had cracked the material into a paper bag, and he did not read the thing before he was in the car. It was printed white on black: 'I am having a nervous BREAKDOWN.' They had been smooth enough to add a Bart Simpson kind of type on the back, but you could tell by the joint in his hardships that he was more than disappointed with this life, and the curl up before his brain-flan was more of a pinkish flute blew from Finland. It was not his type of thing. He never liked the Simpsons.

He was unsure about the shirt whether to wear it or not, but when the other one was smelling, he went for the inside-out type of brand, just to see how that would work. Sally Sparks, her name was underestimating his intelligence. He never thought of her as a person who would need a wheelchair, did you? Well, here he was, working the hallways with no kind of brand, and he had even stopped selling apartments for a while, just to be sure that no more people, in general, would break down the door. He stayed in bed most of the day just to ensure that no one else was coming in that direction.

When she went down to let in the carpenter, he noticed that she had brought him for an interview at the entrance, in the double bed under the books. Or was it just his angle from the top of the stairs? He was not even in his clothes yet; it was afternoon, five o'clock, and he had kept ordering food all day just to have Peter in sight. That was part of the problem; he kept changing his mind all day to keep the 'butler' busy. He had even asked him to give him a massage, due to being a doctor, but Peter had spoken that odd sort of Swahili with a bit of French or whatever they learned in those burned-out countries. He was too hot for his taste; he kept wondering how to have him off work. Then, all of a sudden, at eleven o'clock, he told him that he had to go for lunch, speaking about waffles. He had nearly broiled the guy, but by accident, Sally came back to bed, since he was at home after all, and he accepted the lunch deal, as if he were the one to give the guy his orders. He did not even pay his salary. She asked him about the food; it was stored up on plates all over the room, and he had to tell her that he was a hungry guy. She noticed, she said, but he asked her to stay off the ham on the toast; it could kill her due to the heatwave on the outside; it had ruined the air conditioner in the room, and as she remembered, he reminded her while his hand was moving on her body that Buddha died from a piece of rotten meat. He did not want to do that to her, he said. Did he? He was not exact about it. She had told him about Buddha himself. Not to mention Edvard Munch.

She turned with a sigh.

Welcome to the West Banks

Dora did not have much of a life on her own, did she? So she got really surprised when he asked her out on a ball. He had pretended to be wheeling his wife around in the apartment all day as if he were her nurse and not her husband. Such a Heathcliff! Luckily, Barbara, on her side, had her own fixed cinema date with whoever was taking her to the relatively new James Bond movie, *No Time to Die*. There was no problem mentioned due to carrying her up two floors in a wheelchair, who would make a cinema hall on the first floor anyway in the ages before elevators, or who would order tickets on the balcony when she had to be carried up the stairs. Dora had speculated on the problem for days; not having seen the cinema herself, she was wondering how on earth Barbara had got around to such an appointment. Barbara would not even define what theatre was lounging the film, strangely enough, so Dora even wondered if the theatre existed.

She did not really think that it had been a good idea to accept the invitation. She thought that Barbara would have liked to go herself. Besides, she found it a bit surprising that he actually invited her while she was on her way to the toilet; Barbara could not have seen it, and she felt awkward to mention it. Spending her days in a wheelchair was enough to keep an eye on the thresholds. She did not say a word. She ordered a babysitter for Mitch; he knew the girl next door and prepared for a week, every evening, coming home late due to starting her days at two—such a waste of hours to start that late. She was glad she had the cleaning up at the school in the mornings; she had handed him off being the first child in the kindergarten every morning nearly since birth. At nine o'clock, she started curling up her hair, making the makeup come around, selecting pink for the eyeshadow after having tried out yellow on Monday, and light blue on Tuesday. Wednesday was absolutely earth, and then she glammed Thursday; it was too much with gold, even though she had heard that Sally Sparks had a large house and was celebrating the reopening of the Living Room Area. It was supposed to be splendid. Two newspapers had already mentioned it, referring to an old article from eight years ago.

The whole atmosphere seemed strange, and she was stressing herself every day when she had to go to the toilet, being afraid that he would pass her up again. It kept smelling waffles in the whole house. God knows what sort of lunches Barbara made for herself; there was not a day without that gloomy, fried, spray-fat smell stirring through the rooms. She felt like puking for the first half hour till she got used to the thing. Still, she had to clean off all items back in her own miniature apartment, just knowing that she would not live the night through if she had to endure the fat odour in her own living areas. And her son kept asking what she had been eating.

No one could really save her. Raoul had packed his suitcase years ago; it was not actually a leather outwear, but more or less a paper box of no real measurements; he only kept his underwear in there anyway and a couple of stiff shirts that she prepared for him for those days he would come around. Then his son and wife in Barcelona needed him more often, as if that had not been the case all the time. They always kept needing him there, and he kept talking about Park Guell as if that would be the next place to put in a free Catalonian attack, or whatever the Basks called it. Separatists—or God knows what—those things killed her brain. He sometimes brought back some medical equipment, such as, for instance, the stethoscope. Her son kept listening to her heart long after he was gone. It did not stop beating.

She gave him everything for free; she had such a romantic view of love. She did not even ask him about the ring, which he used the second time they were together, so much waste mentioning the thing when her period had been gone for a month already. She could have gotten rid of the thing, but he was Mitch now, and he would maybe, before he would be 15 or 18, have her travel back to Mexico with success this time. At least, that was the frame she was trying to make for him, and he knew how to do his maths. It took them one hour after eight.

Accidents Do Happen

Gina did not lose her job that often, but Charlie used to lose it a lot before he came to Sally's house. Now he had stayed there for more than twenty years, and it had been a big surprise to him when he lost it due to Peter moving into the small garden house where Gina used to live. Gina, too, lost her job. She did not know why. But when she looked at Charlie's face, it was easy to comprehend. He did not look like he would kill himself anymore.

She did not expect the doctor's son to travel up from Catalonia and find her out on the banks, where she was thinking of ending it too, in the salty water, wondering what pain people were actually describing as an inflammatory response. It seemed so little likely when looking at the cold sea waving at the shore that the wind would ever stop talking about how to deal with the next month, and she was even less likely to ever have a life of her own.

She had met the Catalonian boy before, but she never thought he would move straight into her parents' home; he was not that type. Their house was so small, and she and her brother had shared a bedroom for most of their lives; the extra one was really just for storing things, and it did not even have a window. She remembered that Harry Potter film, the first one; she had not read a book in her entire life; she felt like that poor boy living under a staircase. That was her life at home, but the Spanish boy made her survive because he told her all about having oxygen and water in her lungs the first day they went down to the shore. And she had not even asked him about that question; she was just showing him the surroundings.

His hair was longer, but it was still the same colour, and he did not seem that unhappy anymore. Those days in the guestroom on the third floor in the mansion had nearly killed her; she did not know what to do to make him feel better, but at least she had awakened him every morning at six o'clock so that he would not be late for the hospital. She prepared half a scone and a plain coffee and started to fill a glass of milk on the side, just to see if those proteins would bring forward some colours on his cheeks. It did not.

A Language of His Own

Charlie had never really experienced that much time on his own; he had got one of the rooms up on the third floor for nearly 16 years now. When he was kicked out of his last apartment for not having paid the rent, she just asked him to move in. It was ages ago. The room had a wonderful mid-view, so he could never, looking down in the hallway, taking in all the books on the right wall, ever see her stand talking on the phone in her bare skin tops.

The good thing was that she sometimes came with him to the casino. She taught him how to play slow, and they had gained some millions, but he still liked to make that food, and being called a chef was something he had enjoyed for most of his life, so he kept the job and stored the money. Sometimes he pretended he was out of them, for he actually liked to live there. He was up at five to start preparations for the day, and he always worked at least 12 hours. He did all the bedroom serving by himself, having seen so much moral skin drops in his life that he did not really care about bringing them home to Sally anymore. She was the love of his life, put it the way you want. He stayed as long as she wanted him to.

It was the butler role that was changed. Gina found his face very strange, but he could not explain her the whole thing because he had to move out of the room. When he had prepared his things into some smaller suitcases and was about to talk to her about it, she had lost the house in the garden, and he had nothing to say to her other than how sorry he was. He postponed the car for a week, trying to show how much he would have liked her to stay, but by the end of day three, she had moved out.

It was not really a problem to carry his few items down to the basement. He had carried so many things for himself up and down the stairs for years; he loved to avoid the elevators, serving the food at her bedside, and it had not really been a problem till that guy Wayne came around; he complained about the heat.

The Carpenter Came in Late

Peter did not want to serve in the hallway, but they told him that was part of his job now. He had explained that to Charlie in the Kitchen when the coffee was ordered, with the biscuits on the side. He had cried out to him: “But it is lunch time. I never serve at this time!”

“Two hours off in the middle of the day is not a human right,” Charlie, who was still the chef, had told him in that cold, plain manner he had got as a habit.

The carpenter had not come around till three o’clock; then the coffee was already cold, and he had eaten one of the biscuits himself. For the first time, he really got annoyed by the gloves; he looked like an old, stupid movie serving white guys off the plates. He was thinking about revolution.

The carpenter was very young, not yet thirty; he brought the crystals himself. It seemed strange; he was not even in the electrical department, so who was to fix the electricity? And the lamp itself was very small for the house; he knew this even though he had not once visited the living room area. Sally ate most of her meals to the left in the hallway or in the kitchen on the table that they often used for preparations before lunch. He could still see from the outside that it was the size of a ballroom or two. And it was large; it was not such a thing as a one-lamp armature kind of thing. He did not spell his worries; it had been just two weeks since they found the Munch in the garbage can and less than a month since she discovered the thing on the outdoor marked, claiming it to be his finding. And he could really need the money, so much was for sure.

A Walk in the Park

The lady in the wheelchair seemed to come to the park every day. It was not likely that she was serving that many waffles by accident. First, he had seen her on her own; no wonder he was surprised; she seemed to walk a dog. Second, she kept calling the dog Sparks, and that was what had made him turn around in the first place. Not many people wore that name.

She had a beautiful face. It was difficult to tell her age, but he noticed that she was married and that the wheelchair seemed automatic. It was in a glimpse of an eye before he had to return home to prepare for dinner. Peter was all alone in there, serving coffee in the hallway.

The Living Room Area

He had not seen her in ages, so he did not really want to say no when she asked him to take down the crystals in his mother's kitchen. She always wanted a different lamp, she said to him, and he kind of pretended that it was the reason for his demounting the thing. But he had four weeks or so off work; he had not told her that he was coming to England anyway. He was not a student anymore.

What to Wear on Invitations

When he called about the lamp, Dora told him that she did not really know where he lived in Barcelona. How could she really have been over there? She could not even afford to go to Mexico, and he told her that she was the only lover he had ever had except his wife, and she was the only person he could think of doing such a horrendous thing. She had been that type from the start. He could not even find his great-grandfather's watch after the last visit, but he did not want to mention it to her; that was what had taken him so many years.

Vanity Fair

The magazine came around for the ball, but Sally had been careful to invite them after dark, and she had insisted on having the rooms lightened by candles so that the splendour would gradually be relived on different close-ups. She had explained that metaphysical connection in a way only a philosopher could do, out in the cottage in the garden, to where she had taken the journalists and Pierce Channing so that the guests would not interfere in the conversation. That is why they only had a few minutes on the inside of the ballroom, and they were not likely to be surprised in such a short time.

The Fairytale Princess

Dora had to go to the ball on her own because Wayne did not ever come around; she knew the evening before already. She still decided to make his company, not thinking about the change, but then on her own. So much preparation would not blow into the air. Due to the strange feeling of being left on her own in front of such a mansion, she was already late and had seen masses of people arriving at the property before she did hide in the garden behind some of the rather well-shaped bushes. She was wondering how much was spent on figure-shaping those green plants. She saw a whole bunch of people going towards a small hut in the middle of the garden field. The moonlight seemed to arrange for its presence, and no light was needed for the garden. It was a full moon.

She had not intentionally joined the group, but some of the journalists were so close to her China dress, bought in the market at Piccadilly Circus, and she was afraid that one of them, smoking a cigarette (who would do such a thing these days?) would light a fire in the poisonous material that made the layers of the skirt, and then she would be in full flames before she had even entered the building. It had been on sale for three pounds but looked like a million, which was true.

Those other guys seemed to ask all sorts of questions, but she did not have that interest. She looked at the lady, having heard about her before, and before she really knew it, yesterday's phone call popped into her mind. She put it straight forward, as if she were one of them: "How many lovers have you really had?" And to her wonder, that made the headline for the whole magazine. In addition, she was at the centre of the cover photo in her white China dress, looking like a fairytale princess on the side of a bunch of pens, with that famous Pierce Channing to the right of the picture and Sally Sparks in a rather small armchair between them. Her green silky dress was stretching from the journalists to her legs, making a splendid light show in the electric light in the cabin. She was just a little bit yellow in the face. It was not really her fault; such lightbulbs do sometimes have that effect; that is what most people don't know.

When to Use a Bridge

He wheeled her up the bridge that Sally had made on top of the stairs; it was the only thing she had needed a carpenter for. Barbara had postponed the cinema date, or he did not know if there ever had been one, but she said that the guy bringing her had to work irregular hours. It was a problem to go when no one could carry her up the stairs. He did not really think that much about it since he already had that much to think about; he just knew without saying that when the bridge was clear, he would have to use it, or it would be over.

He was sad to tell Dora, the cleaner girl, that she could not come, for he knew she had prepared for a week, seeing her with different eyeshadows those days he had been in the house. He did not really like to pass her up in the hallway, pretending to be that sort of guy who passes people up like that in their own houses. He felt stupid about it. It looked like she felt uncomfortable too. She was not really going to the toilet anymore. He guessed that the situation for a lone mother was not that easy to manage; she probably had two or three jobs. Her face was nice, but her eyes were a bit underlined, sort of *The Addams Family*-like. What to do with people who slept half of ordinary people? He used to be like that himself till he started staying in Sally's house, and now he was totally eating all meals on her budget. He did not have time to work. There were so many things going on in there. He had to prepare for every type of situation. He had even installed a workout room in the basement, in case she would call his body a problem. He had it for weeks till Charlie moved down to that exact room, pretending to have lost his job. But it was just that butler thing due to Peter taking over, he guessed, and he was right. He just noticed that Gina thought him sacked; then she was sacked too.

God knows what Sally was thinking about. She moved so fast anyway. Before getting to know that Charlie was still in the kitchen, he had stopped working out, eating a whole lot of plates in the bedroom.

He placed Barbara by the fireplace, which was lit to the full; it was really burning some flames in there, but she thought the heat was awful, and he had to move her into one of the corners with all those candles in the window frame. She insisted on staying in a chair with one foot on top of the other while he fetched her a drink and some canapés. He had to bucket her around to the chair at first; he did not really feel like making her sit like a walker, but there was not much choice if he did not want to argue. There were so many people in the room, and he had no idea where Sally would be. He only had the feeling that it would be an idea to really keep the wheelchair, but then Barbara had her will too. It was a bit of a challenge, and she smelled of waffles, still after Dora had bathed her, as if she had sprayed her skin and hair with that particular spray fat after cleaning. She was blank, and she looked really good from a distance. It was the close-up that was the challenge; he could not stand the smell, and Dora had the same problem. She pretended to be nice, wishing her a wonderful time at the ball, which was really something after hearing about the change of invitation while she was washing the dishes. He noticed that she did not lift her face and that a couple of waterdrops seemed to plump from her face down into the soap bubbles and disappear into the white scum that made everything she did that clean and neat. She spent half an hour on some plates and glasses, and when she finished, her face looked professional. Walking them off to the door on the actual night, as they were leaving the house, she had been a bit pale, looking like she wanted to throw up, and she seemed to hold her breath. That was probably why she was so white in the face.

Barbara had overdone it with the perfume too.

Pierce Channing

Pierce placed himself by the woman in the corner; she was the only thing not moving in the room, and he felt a bit dizzy. There was so much out of hand that he did not really know what to do. He tried to see if he could get an eye on Sally after that horrendous interview. Who was that woman in white? God knows she could have learned to keep her mouth shut. She had sort of stolen the show. The blitz did run all over her. He did not know the photographer; it would be impossible to stop that shit from going; he was placed in the middle of it himself. He prayed to God that it would not kill his reputation. He had claimed to be one of Sally's lovers himself a decade ago, just to get into the spotlight. When you want to be a publisher of his kind, you need to stay by some stipulated facts, and that would be: for one, selling needs a bit of a twist, and two, don't touch the obstacles. Freedom of speech was what he claimed it to be. Hanging on her side out at the Globe for a week had given him sort of that go. He was on the front page of every printout in the country. Then he started to publish her works. It was his idea. They called her brilliant—more brilliant than she was before.

The boy in the yellow dress had been observing him for some time. He did not know whether to ask him over; he was beautiful, with that Spanish type of look. He kept pretending to talk to the woman in the chair next to him while he was continuing to observe him, but he did not really know what to say. There was something off with her position; she seemed to concentrate just to sit ordinary on a chair. He did not want to miss out on the boy, so he could not really offer her a drink; it would make him walk away from it all. He said something randomly about the candles; she answered back that it was overwhelming her. He noticed the smell when she talked, or was it her head moving? Waffles—it was too much. He could not really ask if she had been making waffles in the kitchen earlier that day, but it was the only thing going on in his mind. Then the boy, dressed in yellow, was such a surprise. The gloomy white shirt with trumpets hanging out of the sleeves reminded him of some baroque movie. He guessed that he would have his place on the front cover somewhere due to that outfit. He still did not know what comments to make on the house. And he did not dare ask the waffled woman on his side. It would be too much if she would tell him the truth.

He was surprised when the boy came by. He thought he was leaving, and he felt like he had that sort of disappointment that led to a dropped facemask, and then the boy returned from the room next door, and he became surprised. He had not really been in that room after the seance in the cottage out in the garden with the figure bushes so strangely cut. He still had that wondering what would happen next feeling squeezing around in his upper department. He was not really sure how much he could drink; he might not ever get out of the bottle. Then the boy handed him a drink—some pink kind of shit with a grape in it—and a sort of umbrella. Old-fashioned. So out of fashion, it could be in again. He did not really know what clubs Sally frequented these days. Could be all kinds of stupidity; she used to like to dance or float around more likely. *Did you really think that economy meant nothing to her?* the question seemed to gong his brain. It touched a lost area, like the feeling of some random article up in those crumbled hills of the Himalaya. 'The Only Tourist in Bhutan' and then on the picture was Sally. God knows what she was doing up there. He pretended for weeks that he had not noticed. When people asked, he just talked about the mansion and her big project; she was still working on the thing, had plenty to do, and the next novel would be amazing. It took him a year to make it part of her life story—something going on in the mountains, some sky-levelling project. She had met with some famous people up there. They also had some stuff going on as part of being isolated, but they were still creating some shit during the Corona.

He turned towards the boy. "Who are you speaking about? Needing money?"

The boy lifted his glass and clung to his own. "Cheers to Sally! And her renovation project. It is amazing, isn't it?" He opened his mouth but did not know what to say. For the first time in his life, he did not know whether to lean forward or to lean back, and those lips of his, perfectly shaped and still no confusion in that boy's eyes. Was he joking! "When you turn down texts that matters, from so much brighter minds than your own, what do you think the consequences could be?" He did not really have that much of an accent to be a Spanish boy. From Barcelona, he hoped not. Astonishing architecture and all that kind of shit, first. The fireplace was really entering his whole figure; it was perfectly well-shaped, as if he were doing more of a workout than necessary for his type of look. He was beautiful, whatever turn his face would take, and he did not look like killing time; he was in there for a reason, he guessed. He seemed to have an overview of the room. Gaudi, wasn't it! That was the guy, from that town; he should say something about it. He had not expected Sally to come by in her overwhelmingly green dress as well; it was more than too long for her; it had completely blended in with the garden bushes when they were out there. She was like a strange appearance, all of a sudden standing next to the boy. When he rose from the floor, next to him, leaving him with his own impression of Barcelona, was when he first noticed her. Sally, Sally Sparks, on the side of that young gun. In green. Like a whole garden plant on her own. The boy turned towards her, looked at her, and then he kissed her like the evening was over for all of them. Which it most likely was!

Raoul

Before he really had the chance to think about what flight to catch, he was already on his way to the airport. He told himself that it was the crystals and that it was enough. Now, he had not expected her to be on the front cover of Vanity Fair! She was dressed in a white, fluffy meringue; she looked like a wedding cake. The heading was totally off. 'How Many Lovers Have You Had?' He did not even want to know. It had been so many years, and he had really just forgot about her, a Mexican waitress, or what it was. He just loved the way she moved; he never expected her to walk him to his room, their first night, claiming that she had never done such a thing in her life. For sure!

He could not get a hold of the magazine. Impossible to find, down at Las Ramblas, so he thought he might as well head for London while it was still on the shelf. He had just strolled through his Facebook account when some random commercial gave her figure away. It added to the lamp, so to speak. He never liked flying much; everybody knew that; it was the reason for him being twice back in London. After that, he just stayed with trains, asking to have Italy for research, even though his son used to say he should have chosen Greece. So much melancholy in that boy! His wife did not really go out that much anymore, a change of patterns due to finding a small letter in his wallet. God knows what she was doing in his pockets in the first place, but that was what happened. He tried not to think about it; it was really just her lips shaped on a small papercut. It was from the first morning; she got up at five, and he awoke when she was dressing, hearing the whispering noise of her skirt passing her nylons. He lay watching her, and then she noticed, making that swing before she put on the lipstick. She bent over and kissed one of those stamped letter sheets with the hotel's brand on it, turned towards him and said, "Remember me by my lip prints, will you?" He asked her to stay and take the day off and invited her for breakfast; to his wonder, she was fluent in Spanish.

Rafael

The thing is, he was an abused child. He did not count his blessings the way other people did when he got out of Rome on that first occasion. He never wanted to go back. Getting out of that place, had probably saved his life or whatever people found important! He was happy when his father first chose London for his next period of research. That much for London; his father was pale for a week before going, and he bought his Valiums down at the pharmacy, kept speaking about the advantages of trains and cars and kept reading about aerodynamics. He must have thought that he could actually change doing his research on flights and inventions every night. It lasted for a year at the height, and he and his mother never came around to actually visit the place. After the year, his father changed his favourite artist, from Leonardo da Vinci to Caravaggio, and he, which was the hardest thing to forgive, continued to travel to Rome.

He did not really meet her. He just found her looking at him, as if she could measure his whole outfit at a glance. He just immediately knew that he had seen those eyes before, and he remembered that as an incident long ago, looking at Vanity Fair down at Las Ramblas; she had that mansion, a real big house in London, and they were doing a makeover. It was the cover of all times; her dress had been matching the wallpapers. It all looked like the old handcraft, handmade drawings, unique. He could not recognise the patterns. It was at the beginning of his medicine studies; he still dreamt about being an architect, that much for sure, but there was no real reason to break the line. He grew up with his mother telling about the tram accident where Gaudi was hit and died; she just emphasised the idea of sleeping in a small hut at the back of an unfinished site for years, just to see the thing through and then before finishing leave for heaven yourself. He was allowed to run down for construction whenever he wanted, staying that close to it, but he had to promise never to dream about becoming an architect himself, that much for being broke the most of her childhood life, her mother's father was too much of a dreamer, and still, there were copies of all sorts of constructions, even those inverted scale models for the cone-shaped towers of the Sagrada Familia he kept in the living room. He learned it all at his grandfather's apartment, in that small room that was a kitchen, bedroom and living room baked into one; later, he learned it in the museums.

Sally was around for a book launch thing, she told him, but it was during the Corona period. No one was coming anyway; she was on her own in front of the camera. He was the third guest, having written a small essay on the architecture of lungs, which became highly relevant due to the crisis. In meeting with the death of his beloved grandfather, heavy on breathing, lying in his coma, in a public hospital, stored like those thousands of others all across the world. He had to make sure that the mask was on every time he came around. He himself was totally disinfected, wearing a plastic window before his face, gloves and a hospital outfit, and the only one in the family being allowed to visit him due to being in his studies. It had been too much; it was not only the sadness that it was his grandfather lying there; it was the way it all became so linear, impersonal and sad. He overtook the small, crowded apartment and stayed there till Sally came around.

She told him that she had read the article and wondered how those lungs would work in the real world. He answered that she could test it herself. They did not say much more; he walked her to the apartment on the Las Ramblas, not far from where he first saw her on that cover magazine. She asked him if he had any Corona restrictions, and he answered back that he had none if she had none. Then he kissed her in the elevator.

She paid him 200 euros for helping him out with a small article, first time he heard the name Pierce Channing. He felt like a prostitute, but took the money so she might see him again. She was a hundred times his age and he did not expect her to stay more than a day, probably longing to forget about it all. It had happened so fast. They had some common acquaintances, she informed. He felt like seeing them after she had gone, wearing the money in a small pocket on the inside of his dress, as if was going to bring him some luck, starting to dress up for his everyday life. They told him that she left him the key for her Barcelona apartment, that he had promised to fix the wall in the hallway. They did not mention his other job, called him a handy man. He moved in, it was gigantic, bought his first sculpture and placed it in the window. It was the face of Mozart, he thought, but it was in a cubist style.

His Mother

She observed Rafael dismounting the crystals from the kitchen, but she did not really want to blame it on him. Later, when her husband started to mention some unknown forces, having removed the object, she did not say a thing. Then he ordered the ticket for London. She sort of understood what the lamp was about. She packed her things and moved to Rafael's apartment, crowded with her father's things, and found that he had not really been living there for a while. There was nothing in the house except a yellow newspaper with the heading 'The Only Tourist in Bhutan'. She did not know what had kept him for all these years, so heavy with studies and then work that he only came over for sleepovers and dinners. Occasionally, he invited her to the theatre, just the two of them, and took her to the same bar after.

If his sister had claimed the small houseroom, he would have had to sell, but she did not say much, and she only guessed that she was going for the other side, a larger house on the country side. She was living her life in Madrid anyway; who could have known that a head such as that was ever properly worked out in this family—a lawyer in human rights, working for the UN, even helping Sally Sparks with her rights on one of her novels some years ago? She did not say much about it; he had a sister, but people often asked, and they did, whether there was a second child, even though she did not say much back. She just did not want to walk them to Rome. It was such a distance for her too.

Mitch Rembrandt

Mitch did not use his second name much; it was too complicated anyway. People would have laughed if they knew. He was a lonely child, always on his own, almost due to all her working hours. He always missed her, but he easily got friends at school, and when he started dealing with things, he also had some money going. They did the maths for an hour every evening anyway. She did not have to think about his necessities anymore; he had it all and was never hungry. Sometimes he had a babysitter; she came in from the neighbouring apartment. Sandra was nice; she would keep him laughing for some hours, but she made him give away the watch, claiming it was too little salary for the job. And he was that kind of type.

His mother gave him that expensive thing as a gift for his eighth birthday, underlining that everybody in the Alvarez family had a watch for their eighth birthday. He had been proud to wear it. It took him months to run that distance to avoid those boys in class from taking it. Then he gave it away to Sandra, and there was not much to do about it. He kept regretting it, as if the watch had been some sort of an unknown father that could explain all those lonely years. He was still just 12, but he felt like he had been an adult for all his life. He took care of his mother; sometimes he prepared a meal and left it in the fridge for her. He knew how to toast things.

He just did not know how to keep her at home in the evenings. And then she became famous for it.

His Sister

She did not want him to bring around Sally Sparks in the first place, and she did not really feel like seeing him either. He was too much of a kind; they always had to argue about something. He was brighter than her, more fair; he always was, and that was the problem with her type of work. It was difficult to come around to the real measurements; it was all those blows down the balloon, but she did not really change the party. She knew too. He was right about that. Then he wanted her to get in touch with the Street Magazine to make them aware of the consequences of the financial crises; she did not feel like it, but she owed him one. While she was taking the phone, she felt like she was finally seeing them, and she noticed without much surprise that the two of them were having an affair. Her brother, believe it or not, was actually in love. To her surprise, with a woman his mother's age! Still, she was difficult to define. That was what surprised her even more.

She had Sally do her signature on a couple of copies of her last book, 'Before the Mountains', so she could pass them on for Christmas; it was not yet September, but what a heck. Famous for being particular and on time, she even went with her father to Rome for three years; after that, she did not feel like coming home. Barcelona had changed. She guessed it was due to London.

Sally

She would not have asked Frida for help if Pierce Channing had not insisted on taking half of her royalties for the last book, claiming sales to be the real work. She could not afford it. Frida took her in, like in the old days before the accident, and turned on the crystal lamp in the kitchen and made her supper. She knew what soup she liked, so she did not say much, having nothing really to add, being inside her house in London for the last year writing by herself was finally back in Barcelona. They had a glass of wine, and she was, of course, due to the restrictions, the only guest in the house. Frida had not been out for weeks after losing her dad to the horrible disease. It nearly killed her when she mentioned Rafael and his amazing effort to keep that emotional old man in balance, even through his worst moments, craving for air. She had brought the church model over, and the cones were hanging from the ceiling in a corner of the living room; she wished she could have placed it there before, even decades before so she could have learnt about the architecture of air a bit sooner.

She had not expected him to be at home, there was so much to do at the hospital, passing her in the living room when she watched the model. So much for common acquaintances! He was made in the house. Frida, his mother, recommended his sister again, in Madrid, a human rights lawyer, if she wanted to publish the article, He came with her and said she could need some company on the way. His mother did not want him to. They drove his father's car, both wearing masks. His father was delayed in Rome anyway.

Dora

She had not expected the dress to catch fire, but that much for standing too close to the fireplace. It was fast, so fast that there was nothing much to do. The African butler who had been in an intense conversation with some professor-like type, a short guy in an old-fashioned dress with a grey beard and thick glasses, was still holding the drinks on some silver plate. She could see him turning slowly towards her when the smoke started to catch everybody's attention, and then, with an open mouth, he sort of threw the drinks on her as if the fluids would stop the fire. Then he just pushed her to the ground and rolled her in the floormat; she could smell the old thing that had not been walked on for years. Dust. She did not know how he did the thing, but people pushed away as they, at the glimpse of an eye, got hold of the situation, so all of a sudden, the mat was empty with legs in shoes and pumps, and she was on her own, free to be rolled up in that thing. Anyway, she was already lying there due to having all those drinks bumping on her backside and the pushdown; she did not really know how he did that without catching fire himself. Pain. He rolled her in; she was warm, and she could feel that horrible plastic heat glued into her skin, but the wool rye still had that massive soothing feeling, even though she was wondering about the air; she was kind of tumbled around in a long rocket, and she could not tell whether it was a metre or two to get out of the thing. Then she heard people shout, “You must roll her up; she has no air!”

“Take away your heads from the opening; you are filling in with carbon dioxide.”

“I am a doctor; I am a doctor. Please, will you step aside? Gina, will you get me some water from the kitchen in a clean bowl? See to it that there are some strips of clothing, clean too, would you please?”

When they rolled her up, the boy in the yellow dress was leaning over her, telling her that he needed her to roll over. He asked Sally to use the phone in the hallway section; it might be a bit faster. Some people kept thinking about that long after the party was over, but some had already lifted their mobile phones and were calling 999. The ambulance was on its way. The doctor kept heating her down with water; he said he had to take what he had. He did not tell her it was too large for a small box of gel or some sort of thing that could have freaked her out. He just waited till they carried her out of there; it was evident to all of them that it was impossible to foresee the damage. The dress looked glued to her body, as did the paper umbrellas from the drinks. They were sort of spreading out on the backside. Like a pattern.

She was still conscious and kept thinking about Mitch, repeating his name. Someone asked if there was anyone in there who knew her. She is some sort of journalist, maybe from Vanity Fair, some people said. Then Wayne’s face bent down towards her. “Dora, what are you doing here? Do you want me to come to the hospital?” He seemed to hesitate to ask the question, looking around in the room.

Then she heard on the side, "I'll take Barbara home. I was going to carry her to the movies anyway."

"Ye, if you could do that, you are working irregular hours anyway, aren't you? I think I have her home number, so I can get hold of her son!" He seemed annoyed speaking to the guy, but he assured her that he wanted to come.

She was carried out of the house, but she could still see that Sally had come back and turned off the lights again. She felt strange that the doctor, being a rather young boy, had undressed.

Barbara

Barbara did not know what to say when that guy next to her leaned over and said, “I don’t fucking know what to do; it’s a freak show. I really don’t want to do the launch anymore. I’m fucking out of it.”

“Sorry?” she said. “Launch?”

“Ye, this is the book release for her latest book. After the Mountains. What did you think?”

“Isn’t it a ball?” she asked him.

He stirred at her. “A ball! It was fuckin’ going to be the renovation of the house! God knows where she met that boy!”

“Are you going to interview her?”

“Yes, of course. Why did you think there’s a goddamn fucking scene in there?”

“Oh!” she said. “I haven’t really been in there yet.”

Then the woman in white took fire, and she started to burn out there in the middle of the floor. Suffington threw all the drinks on her, and the umbrellas waltzed through the air. People were shouting and moving away from the carpet that she was standing on. Suffington pushed her down without hesitation and started rolling her inside the mat, trying to take out the flames. There could not be much air in there. Some faces bent down to try to see her down in the tube. Kind of filling the hole, she hoped he would roll her up before it was too late. The guy next to her rose, screaming. “Fuck!” And then the lights came on. The pale, yellow tapestry, sun-bleached and really outworn, gloomed towards them. It was impossible not to notice how little that was done in the room; it was not even cleaned properly. The fireplace was black and outburned; it just did not show when the flames were that high. He sat down next to her again with his mouth open, sweating; he had a handkerchief in his hand that he kept stamping towards his forehead. The doctor undressed, and the whole room kind of exploded. Every eye was on the incident, and when Sally went out to call, they were all watching her too. There was not a word being spilled.

Barbara leaned towards him and whispered: “I can do it.”

“Do what?”

“The interview, if you don’t feel like it!” she said. “I am used to things being awkward!”

He was a shocked that he had to carry her into the next room, but what could he do? When he had accepted her offer, it was kind of too late. Pierce Channing; she did not call him by his name, but everybody knew. He was far too polite to say something when the deal was done. He was even about to pay her for it—500 in cash—For an unprepared book release!

Gina

She spent every day watching him tan; there was not much more to do. Sometimes they talked, but he was very different from her. He had even moved into the room 'under the stairs' sort of, claiming that the windows offered too much light. Then he was about to start working in some weeks, and he would find a place on his own. First, he said, he had to finish the summer course in architecture; it was a weekend sort of thing, which lasted for a month. Next was starting at the Warwick University Hospital, doing his research on how to prevent Alzheimer.

Then she had the call from Charlie if she could come to the ball so that they would have some people to serve during the situation; she could not tell him no. So she went in her traditional outfit and learned from Rafael that he was invited too; she did not believe it much. But to her surprise, he showed her an invitation in an envelope addressed for Spain. He did not say anything more. She came to remember that winter; those months Sally was on her journey in the Himalayas. He spent those weeks up in the guestroom to the right of Charlie's room, up on the third floor. She was looking after him, thought he would leave breathing as an option. He left before Sally returned, and for some reason, she never told her about the stay. It must have been Charlie who brought him in.

She was kind of surprised seeing him in the yellow dress, but she did not speak out her confusion. He matched the rose Sally had asked them all to keep on their right chest side, and she found that strange. All this yellow for a ball. She had not expected him to take off his clothes; she was kind of devastated, and then she had to get the water in the kitchen. Charlie kept observing her. He did not say much, but everything was cleaned and neat in there, as if there had been nothing to prepare for the party. She kept thinking if this was the reason for his tanning all week, Rafael must have expected something to happen. Then she saw them carry that woman whom Wayne had come around with; she had been in a wheelchair. She did not know he was about to bring his own date. She thought him and Sally to be a pair, at least for all those hours alone in her room this past year. Pierce Channing seemed to crumble under the weight, but he was able to put her off in the armchair on the other side of the table. Sally sat already at her side of it all, with her book on her lap. Pierce Channing took the microphone and presented the two of them: Barbara from British News and Sally Sparks, a world-famous author and also a well-known journalist only a few years ago. Gina thought it strange; she went by with a couple of cups of coffee; it should have been tea, but she had learned her line. "Just to quicken you up a bit." That was how her ass came into the 'Al Jazeera', believe it or not. There was still some Arabic interest in Sally's writings, and Gina became aware of that, that same week, when she saw the whole width of her skirt back, and started to work out four times a week, till they called her about the cabin again.

Wayne

He did not know how to stay in equilibrium; he had taken off his shirt, wearing a T-shirt under it with the writing 'I am having a nervous BREAKDOWN'. The hospital staff kept their distance. Seeing the drawing on the backside, they probably kept thinking that he had put her on fire himself. He kept hanging around waiting for Mitch; he felt kind of obligated, knowing that the young lad did not have much of a father. Strangely enough, he liked that young creature; he came with his nanny, a girl his own age, wearing an over-dimensional watch, looking like a family man kind of thing. The boy himself wore a black cotton T-shirt, very much like his own. "You buy it here." He did not know the reference, but it looked okay for him until they went out to take some fresh air, and the boy lit a giant joint in the staircase. Then he decided to hang around till morning, hoping to come back into Sally's place when she woke sometime around midday, but to his surprise, the phone had gone to answering machine when he called around eleven. She did not lift off the handle. He never really got her mobile number. He was tired, taking a cab home from the hospital, but he took a swing around to the mansion, just to tell her how everything had sorted itself out rather well. No one opened the gate before the garden, and he did not feel like climbing the walls in case Peter would see him from the cabin. He decided to wait.

Peter

Peter Suffington arrived at Lampedusa by boat; he never spoke of it. Half of the passengers had left the boat with their lives in their own hands, and only a few rose above the water. He was one of them. He had always been a good swimmer. Then he stayed on the island until he had the possibility of going to Rome. He learned how to sell Colosseums, bought them cheap from another seller and slept every night at the same spot around the train station, usually having an hour awake to watch over those other guys as they did for him. It was a hard mattress, but he learned how to keep warm by staying close enough to the person next to you to feel the body heat. They called him S; having so many nationalities to deal with, he just kept it simple. When the occasion arrived, he took the first train to Paris, hearing that it was possible to succeed if you did it the right way. He had a hard time selling the Eiffel Tower, but by accident, he met Rafael in a café. He asked him to sit down; he sold him a small-scale model for ten times the price, and he promised him to go to London on the ticket he offered him the day after at the spot they had agreed upon. He would apply for a job at Barbara's house. She would need someone to carry her around; she sat in a wheelchair.

After a month or two in her house, he learnt that Wayne was not much at home—nearly ever. He and Barbara had a nice time in the kitchen every day, and he taught her to make waffles, pretending it was something he knew from a hotel he had worked in on the continent. It was the second time he tasted the thing; he always wanted to try it once more. The job at Sally's house was offered him by Pierce Channing; he did not know the guy at the time, but he passed him up in his room one of the days, telling him that there was a butler job, quite well paid, but he had to do an interview. In London, he went by the name Suffington. Barbara found that to be a wonderful Cameroonian first name, and he did not say more. He could not go by S for the rest of his life. Up in the mansion, he arrived at 1200; he did not go to the main entrance, learning that he was to enter at the left, the kitchen entrance. He came straight into the gigantic kitchen to find Charlie, Gina and Sally at the kitchen table. It was first when he put eyes on the old woman, hard to tell her age, that he arrived in himself again; he remembered that he was Peter and why he had travelled in the first place. It took him a week to explain to her about the doctorate, why he had to leave and how important it was for him to learn proper English. Maybe he could get around to it again. He trained with Charlie in the kitchen for fourteen days, and then he started serving in the bedroom, being kind of prepared for it. That was where he met Wayne.

He could have told Barbara that the painting on the cardboard definitively was no Munch, but he did not, probably she knew it herself. It was not signed. *The Scream* was a very different image; it was not so that it was without value; it was just very clear that it was an Egon Schiele and that it did not scream much. When Wayne threw it in the trashcan, it was quite clear to both of them that he did not know much about art. He ruined part of the red, having some fat on the cardboard; it would be impossible to fix due to it being cardboard paper, already a horrible material thinking about the acid in the material. He read about it for a night, finding no ways to save the corner; it would have to stay as it was, maybe just drying it out with some natrium chloride, but it would still stay darker, he guessed, but not ruin the thing entirely.

He got around to English quite well in the period when Wayne was out selling houses. There were some hours in the morning when they worked on the grammar, and he tried to learn 10 words a day. When the book launch came around in August for 'After the Mountains', he learnt that he had to serve with the white gloves on. He met Rafael again while he was building the bridge on the stairs for wheelchair users. He did not know that he was a carpenter, and he did not really say much after seeing him that first day, more than two hours late in the hallway section with some crystals. A lamp, far too small for those big rooms. And Rafael was not even an electrician.

He saved the woman in white and was invited over by Wayne to have a 'thank you' at the hospital. He had joined them there for an hour or so, seeing that Wayne was a bit pale; he had not really seen him back at the house for a while before the ball or after.

When he was at the spot, Rafael came around to see Dora too, having heard that it was open for visitors. He had not really been aware that the guy was really a doctor till that incident with the fire. While they were sitting in the hallway, Mitch, her son, arrived with a small girl a little under his age, maybe, who claimed to be his babysitter, preparing his meals. He had a T-shirt with the writing 'You buy it here'. The girl had a watch over dimensioned for her hand that caught the young doctor's attention. "It looks like my great-grandfather's watch!" he said to her and wondered if she could show him the thing. She took it off, and the initials engraved in the silver plate on the backside were the same. After that, Rafael went into the room. Peter was still waiting for his turn, having to know how her overall condition was first. Another Spanish guy arrived, claiming to be a doctor too. He was very much alike Rafael, strangely enough. He had to sit down and wait; the nurses had not seen him before.

The new arrival had a short glimpse at Mitch, looking at his T-shirt and asking what he did sell. Mitch brought out a big, white plastic bag from his trousers with marihuana, asking, "Do you want some?" The guy jumped in his seat and asked him to put it back immediately in his pockets, asking about his name instead. The boy said, "Mitch Rembrandt Alvarez." The last one seemed a little strange, and the guy on the side became a bit white in the face. He sat with his mouth open and did not say much. When he saw the girl on the side, he just rose, took her hand and started to loosen her watch.

"It is my father's watch!" he said, turning towards Peter as if he could understand the problem. "Did you not have it on your eighth birthday?" he said, sitting down next to Mitch again. The boy did not say much, leaning his face on the man's shoulder. Then he started to cry.

Sally was not supposed to arrive at the sight, but she came by too. She carried a pink bag, claiming it to be some leftovers from the party a couple of days ago, meant for Dora in there. She did not want to visit her herself, so she handed it over to

Wayne after saying hello to the Spanish guy who was still trying to comfort the boy on his shoulder. "Long time, no see, Raoul!" They shook hands, then she left the building. Soon after, Wayne left too, without the bag. When Peter returned to the mansion some hours later, the gate was locked; he did not want to climb the wall, guessing that Gina had moved back into the cottage during those hours. He went home to Barbara. They were eating waffles when the postman arrived with the mail—even a letter for him—welcoming him to a preparation course in English for University. Some would have said it was a bit late.

Charlie

Charlie did not want to go with them to the MET when the invitation for the reopening came around. Sally liked to bring them all occasionally; she was famous for it. He said he would watch the house, and Gina said so too. Then they would finally have some time on their own again. Sally still wanted to go, she said, to watch the next performance by one of the best artists in the world; it had been quiet for too long. She loved Marina Abramovitsj. It would be a wonderful celebration.